Bikes

Look at the bikes.

These bikes are good
for racing.

These bikes are good

for riding on rocky ground.

These bikes can carry

two people.

These bikes have
hand pedals.

These bikes stay still
when you ride them.

Some people do tricks

on bikes. Wow!

Look at this bike.
What parts can
you name?